The Bunny Who Found Easter

To Steve, who gave me the idea
—C.Z.

To Crumb, who arrived with the rabbits
—H.C.

Text copyright ©1959 and © renewed 1987 by Charlotte Zolotow
Illustrations copyright © 1998 by Helen Craig

www.houghtonmifflinbooks.com

Library of Congress Cataloging-in-Publication Data

Zolotow, Charlotte.
The bunny who found Easter / by Charlotte Zolotow ;
illustrated by Helen Craig.
p. cm.
Summary: A lonely rabbit searches for others of his kind from summer
through winter until spring arrives and he finds one special bunny.
RNF ISBN 0-395-86265-5 PAP ISBN 0-618-11127-1
[1. Rabbits—Fiction. 2. Easter—Fiction.] I. Craig, Helen, ill. II. Title.
PZ7.Z77Bs 1998   [E]—dc21 97-36827   CIP AC

Manufactured in China
WKT 20 19 18 17 16 15 14 13 12

The Bunny Who Found Easter

Charlotte Zolotow

Illustrated by

Helen Craig

Houghton Mifflin Company

Boston

One day a little bunny woke up from a
long nap alone under a tall elm tree.
He heard the silence of the woods around
him and wanted other rabbits like himself
for company.

"Can you tell me where I will find other rabbits?" he asked a sleepy old owl in the elm tree.

"Other rabbits?" said the owl, "Why there are always rabbits at Easter."

"Where is Easter?" asked the little bunny eagerly.

But the old owl had dozed off to sleep again in the bright sun.

"It must be some place to the East," thought the bunny and he set off searching.

It was a hot summer day. The leaves in the trees stood as still as a painting against the blue sky. The bunny found a pool of water, and down in the water silvery trout flashed by. But there were no bunnies about.

"Then this can't be Easter," he thought, and went on his way.

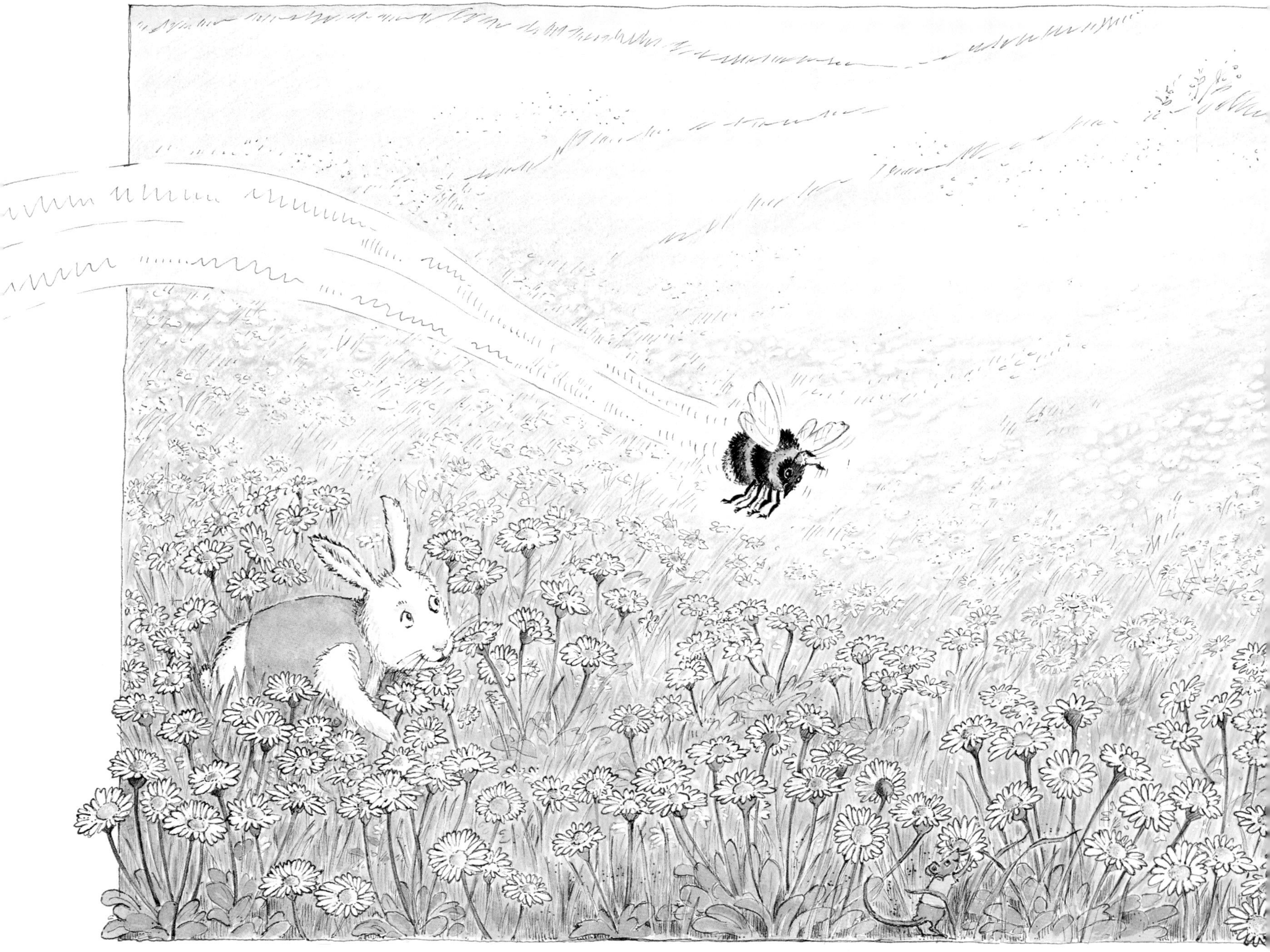

He came to a field full of daisies. There was a hot summer daisy smell over the field and the bunny's nose twinkled. A big slow bumblebee hummed by. But in all that whiteness of daisies there was no whiteness of bunnies like himself.

"This isn't Easter," the bunny said, and he went on.

Once he was caught in a summer storm. The sky looked like night. Suddenly a streak of lightning, the color of the stars, forked through the sky. Great rumblings rolled from one end of the world to the other. The rain came down so fast that the bunny could hardly see the mountain laurel just ahead.

Slowly the rumbling rolled by.
Slowly the sky brightened.
Slowly the rain stopped.

He could see the
mountain laurel with
the wet shining leaves,
each flower cup filled
with one sparkling
drop of rain.

But he couldn't see any other bunnies shaking the rain off their wet white fur.

"Not Easter," he said sadly, and hurried on his way.

Summer was nearly
over. The leaves on the
forest trees began to
turn, brown and gold
and red.

Dead leaves crackled
under the soft rabbit hops
of the little bunny who
was looking for Easter.

He stopped under
a tree to rest and a
round shiny red
apple fell down
and startled him.

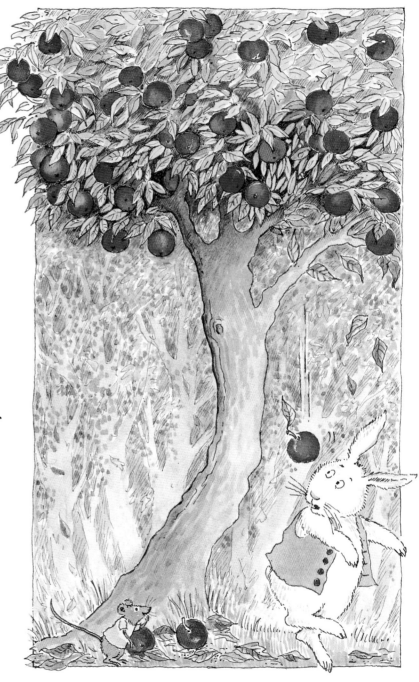

It smelled of autumn
and crispness.
He took a bite with his
two front sharp teeth.

When he had
crunched the apple
to its seeds, he looked
around and sighed.

There wasn't another
bunny to be seen.

One day it began to snow. Soft white flakes drifted down from the sky, and the air was sharp and cold and still. When he hopped through the white drifts he left little dark footprints in the snow. But no matter which way he hopped, his footprints never crossed other bunny footprints. The little bunny was alone in a world without rabbits.

There were birds, little black sparrows like ink drops in the snow.

Brown squirrels leaped about in the bare branches of the trees.

Once he saw a whole
family of deer slipping
into the forest at dawn.

But there wasn't another
long eared, pink nosed,
white furry rabbit like
himself to be seen.

"This can't be Easter
yet," he thought, and
his loneliness grew
inside of him.

That night the bunny curled up in a hollow tree to keep himself warm out of the wind and sharp air.

When he woke up the next morning there was something different.

It smelled . . . he quivered his nose and smelled hard . . . it smelled of greenness and warm soft sunlight.

The little bunny felt sure he would come to Easter soon.

In the forest the black twigs had little tight curled green buds. The birds were singing high up in the trees as the bunny hopped ahead looking for Easter.

Suddenly he saw something in the muddy earth that made him stand perfectly still with excitement. Crossing in front of him, and going into the woods where he had never been, were little rabbit paw prints on the ground!

He followed the paw prints very carefully down a hidden path. There, in a clearing, he saw someone small and furry resting on a mossy bank.

It was another bunny!
She had brown fur. She
had long ears like himself,
and eager bright eyes,
like himself.

The little bunny was
so happy to find her,
he completely forgot
about Easter.

Hopping back through
the forest with her,

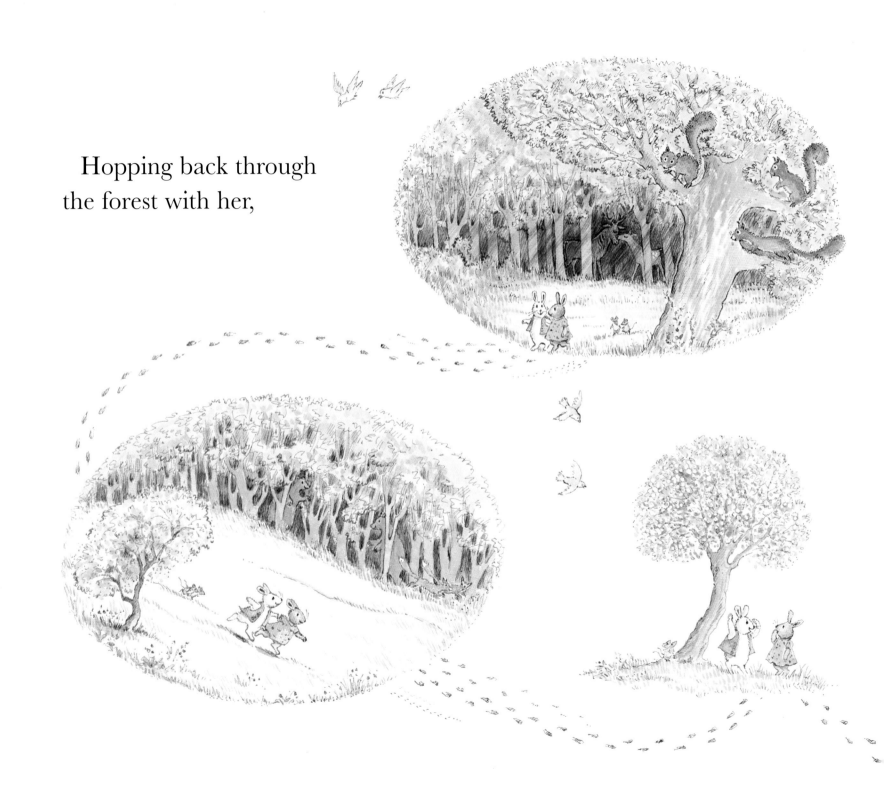

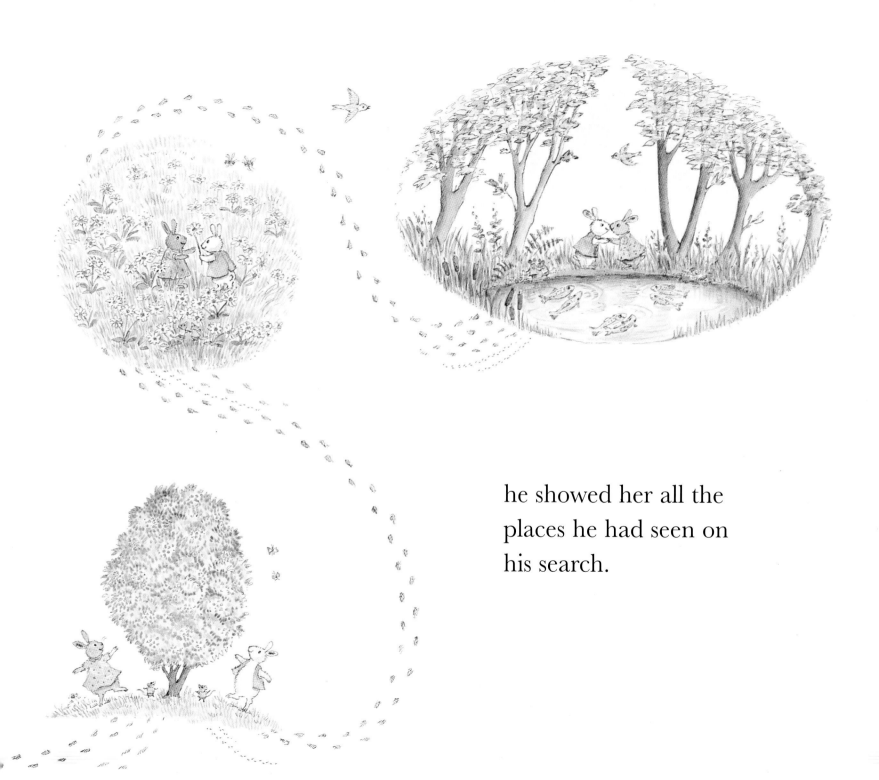

he showed her all the
places he had seen on
his search.

At last they came to the tall
elm tree where he had first
awakened to find himself alone.
But now his loneliness was gone.
The two bunnies were very
happy together.

Soon they had a whole family
of little rabbits, tiny, soft sleepy
things with long sweet ears and
small wet noses. The bunny's
heart throbbed with happiness
at this wonderful earthsmelling
sunlit bunny-filled world.

"Aha!" said the old owl when he saw the bunny's family, "didn't I tell you so? At Eastertime there are always rabbits."

The bunny felt his little bunnies around him and the earth blooming beyond them, and all things growing. And he understood at last that Easter was not a *place* after all, but a *time* when everything lovely begins once again.